Chinatown, Los Angeles. Young men are disappearing from their beds, sometimes vanishing as they cross the street with friends. The few witnesses who actually report a strange, mystical creature, soon suffer memory lapses and die.

Yet the young men all return, one by one. They seem the same, but they are different. Strange things are happening all over Chinatown, as if an odd mist enshrouds it. None of the men who disappeared can say what happened to them.

Late at night, however, this legion of men, in love and lust with the one they call Banpaia, reach out for one another in the frenzy of their need. For Feng Li, a suicidal young man who feels he was saved by the legendary, centuries-old Japanese vampire, yearns for only him. For Feng, there can be only one to claim his body and his heart.

This book is a work of fiction. Names, characters, places, and incidents either are products of the author's imagination or are used fictitiously. Any resemblance to actual events or locales or persons, living or dead, is entirely coincidental.

Banpaia
Copyright © 2020 A.J. Llewellyn and D.J. Manly
ISBN: 978-1-4874-3115-0
Cover art by Martine Jardin

Published by eXtasy Books Inc or
Devine Destinies, an imprint of eXtasy Books Inc

Look for us online at:
www.eXtasybooks.com or www.devinedestinies.com

DEDICATION

For Adam Killian, because he loves vampires

Banpaia
Banpaia 1

By

A.J. Llewellyn and D.J. Manly

CHAPTER ONE

Feng took his time finishing his second cup of coffee at the Korean café on Sixth Street before checking into work for the night shift at the dreary Cedar House hotel. It was late October and LA's weather was still hot. Too damned hot with Halloween only a week away. Not only did the locals say it presaged an earthquake, but it also felt wrong. Very wrong, when the mysterious fog enveloped the whole downtown neighborhood each night.

It was almost five p.m., the sun starting to set. He'd been here two hours. Anything to avoid being home.

The café was warm, but a slight breeze blew in as the front door opened and three guys walked in. The waitress came from the kitchen with a fresh tray of pastries for the counter display. Feng detected the smell of fresh *go mo bang*, the peanut butter-flavored bread he adored. No time. And . . . big inward sigh . . . he shouldn't spend the money.

Feng caught a glimpse of a certain gleaming dark head in the doorway, but the guy wasn't looking at him. Ki was pointing at the sticky buns, laughing with his friends.

Damn. He had to show up right now. Feng hated having to leave. He felt safe here. His evening desk clerk position at the Cedar was the worst job he'd ever had, but he needed it. His dad was still out of work and his mom was drinking heavily. He made sure his head was bent to his ever-present notebook as the three men walked from the front door into the café. He heard movement as they settled beside him at the next table.

Feng stayed very quiet, pen in hand, doodling.

1

"So, anyway . . . they say he just disappeared," the first voice said.

Feng tried to place it. He knew the three guys beside him on sight, but they never invited him to join them, even the nights they all sang karaoke in the upstairs Shelter Room in Little Tokyo. Only one of them ever acknowledged him and that was only after they sang. Sometimes they sang back to back, wowing the crowds. Ki was Japanese and Feng was certain that was the problem. Old country rivalries between the Japanese and Chinese had taken root here in California. The Koreans had it worse. The Japanese street gangs picked on the Koreans. But not this crowd. In this café, they all blended and got along . . . on the surface.

Ki's family lived way down in San Pedro, but Ki had recently moved up here to Little Tokyo. He wanted to be an actor and singer.

Feng closed his eyes, squeezing his pen a little harder. Each little detail he gleaned about Ki was hard-earned and won, like little nuggets of gold after a long day panning for the stuff. He had such a fierce crush on Ki. He liked everything about him; the man's smooth, milky-colored skin, his long, dark hair, his absolutely spectacular voice.

"What do you mean disappeared?" another voice asked.

"They were crossing the street. They stepped off a curb. Joby says he heard a car stop but didn't look because they were crossing legally. By the time he got to the other side, Vince was gone."

There was a moment of hushed silence.

"Nah . . . I don't believe it." This came from Ki. Feng recognized his cadence. He'd had a crush on the guy for six months now, so he was used to the ache, but today, it hurt.

Today it hurt worse than ever because Feng's mom had disappeared the night before and both he and his dad had been secretly relieved.

Maybe the mysterious vampire would take her, too . . . only most people didn't believe in the vampire. Feng did. He heard the whispers, felt the tremor of fear. He'd prayed once or twice for the vampire to claim him. He liked hot, young guys. Maybe Feng wasn't hot enough. He cradled his cup between both hands. One more sip and he had to be on his way.

"Joby says Vince's family is frantic," the first voice said again.

"Vince disappeared in broad daylight!"

Sixteen men had vanished so far. Most disappeared from their bedrooms, one from a crowded elevator and now . . . this Vince guy.

"Nah, I don't believe it," Ki said again. "Somebody's trying to spook everyone because it's almost Halloween."

Feng had heard this plausible story before, but the vanishings started a few weeks ago. The first one was right here in Little Tokyo, or J-Town, as most people called it. The vampire had crossed the invisible demarcation zones between J-Town, Koreatown, and Chinatown. Feng lived in Chinatown on Hill Street, above the seafood dim sum café that could never get better than a C rating from the Health Department and was frequently shut down for code violations.

He'd slept many nights with his window open hoping for abduction. Hoping he took the mystery vampire's fancy. Nah, Ki was right. Vampires weren't real. His mother's explanation of kinky sex abductions or maybe even secret organ harvesting, made more sense, except . . . *where were the bodies?*

"Look, he's listening," One of the voices said.

Are they talking about me?

This shocked Feng. He longed to turn and look at them, maybe say, *boo!*, but didn't hurry his movements. Even as he felt the weight of the stares on his back and shoulders, he took his time.

"Nah," the second guy at the table said. Feng wished it had

been Ki who'd said it.

He left a buck under his coffee cup, shoving his journal into his backpack. He heard the conversation at the next table resume as soon as he started to walk away. He fully breathed again once he was out of the café. Feng could smell human urine now, but then they were almost at Skid Row here. Vagrants didn't care where they peed. He stood outside, trying to imagine how it would feel if you crossed the road with your best friend thinking everything was okay, only to get to the other side and find he'd vanished into thin air. Freaky, man.

Feng checked the time on his cell phone as he crossed the street. Three minutes to five. The Cedar House stood in a semi-decrepit pocket on the edge of J-Town, right at the crossroads of the downtown Toy District. He liked the many Korean cafes lining Sixth Street, just two blocks from the rundown hotel on Fourth. For a shabby looking, four-story building slapped up against Skid Row, it surprised him how many Chinese tourists came there each month.

Some had sure been sold a bill of goods by their tour promoter. Others were students whose friends back home had fond memories of the Cedar and its cantankerous manager, Mrs. Wei. He bit his lip. He shouldn't call her cantankerous. She was a sweet old thing but lately she was in so much pain from her sciatica she sometimes took it out on Feng.

The truth was the elderly Chinese woman was kinder to him than even his own mother. He blushed with shame thinking about the call he and his father had received from the Commerce casino in the early hours of the morning. Having been banned for life from gambling there, his mom had shown up drunk and caused a scene. She was now at home, sleeping it off. He wondered who had it worse, him or his dad. As he rounded the last corner and opened the door to The Cedar House, he decided his dad had it much, much worse. His mom when she was drunk, was bad. Mom hung-over was a friggin' nightmare.

Mrs. Wei greeted him with a wide smile and an old-worldly tilt of her head. She might have been the proprietress of a high-class joint, the way she greeted him and their guests. *Guests!* Man, some of them were total losers.

He was right on time. He never liked to give up more time to the Cedar than he had to. She buzzed him behind the oak and glass door into the office enclosure. He checked the books. Six new guests. He recognized three of the names. They got a lot of repeat business here. It wasn't that their services were so fantastic. It was that the hotel's close proximity to many homeless shelters made this a second home to many abuse victims.

New laws passed by California's governor no longer gave long term housing to men and women residing in shelters. Every thirty days, these long-term homeless had to leave their shelters and find someplace else to stay for a week. During that time, they had to reapply for their emergency housing and with Mrs. Wei's help on the computer, they left again, safe from the streets or abusive spouses, to wait out another month in secrecy.

It broke his heart to see Angie Montoya's name on the register. She and her eleven-year old son, Antonio, had fled her abusive husband. It had taken some resilience on her part considering he'd beaten and tortured her, knocking out all her teeth. Now with the state's help, she was taking computer courses and would soon be eligible for permanent housing which she would subsidize with her new income, once she landed a job.

People like Angie and the unsuspecting travelers who'd been duped into booking at the Cedar were the ones who got under Feng's skin. He worried about them. They were like a second skin he couldn't shed.

"Here, Feng, I have a little gift for you," Mrs. Wei said.

She handed him a red envelope. It was an especially pretty one with a golden dragon and the red lanterns so popular in Chinatown.

He turned it over in his hands. "A *lisee*? For me?"

She smiled. "I know it's your birthday in a couple of days. I'm giving this to you now."

"Oh, but—"

She knew. The new *Dragon Ball manga* would be coming out at midnight and he'd coveted it. Wow . . . he'd missed the last few issues. He could maybe even buy back copies.

Mrs. Wei shook a finger at him. "This is for *you*. Hide it from your mother. And under no circumstances are you to pay any bills with it. Understood?"

He stared at the envelope, feeling its thickness. Tears stung his eyes. Even as he felt the need to protest, he felt the wind blowing away from those sails. He traced the fire-breathing dragon with his fingertips. She'd found him the perfect envelope.

"I want you to believe in hope," she said. "Hope is all we have in this world, Feng."

I'm going to be twenty-two, he realized. Twenty-two, but I feel like forty-two.

"Thank you, Mrs. Wei." He felt humbled by her generosity and her compassion. He didn't open the *lisee*. He didn't care how much was in it. Her thoughtfulness really counted with him. She was right, though. As much as he loved the envelope, which was a tradition in the Chinese culture, if his mom went through his stuff, which she regularly did, and she saw the *lisee*, she would know somebody had given him money.

She would demand it, claiming bills needed to be paid, when he was the one who paid all the bills. His beautiful gift would be swallowed up by a poker machine as soon as his mom got her hands on it.

He kept the envelope on him all evening. He kept touching

it in his jacket pocket. Mrs. Wei must have known how much it meant, because he caught her smiling at him a couple of times.

At six p.m. Mrs. Wei was supposed to leave but still she stayed, fussing over guests, worrying about little details. It was what made her a great manager, but she needed to take a break. Feng wished her cherished and adored daughter would spend more time with her. Instead, he frequently heard Mrs. Wei saying, "No, problem, I understand," when her daughter called to cancel their evening plans.

"What are you going to do with your evening?" he asked.

She smiled at him.

"Are you going to trip the light fantastic and go dancing with some fancy man?"

She laughed. "Trip is right. I'm so tired, I'd fall over fast."

Mrs. Wei had been a celebrated *ta ge* dancer in her day. Now, she hobbled. It was amazing how much she achieved on an average day, even when she was in pain. He'd once found footage of her, strangely enough, on YouTube, in an old competition. She'd been as surprised as he, to see how beautiful she had been when she was young. Her feet had mesmerized him. He'd never seen actual *ta ge* dancing before and the ancient Chinese art of step-dancing had been lyrical, beautiful to watch.

"Get going," he said now, keeping his voice gentle.

"You trying to get rid of me?" she feigned a scowl. The truth was, he knew, she liked the show of attention that Feng gave her.

"Before I leave," she said, holding up a crooked finger, "there is some food I couldn't quite finish, so please eat it so the food doesn't spoil."

He swallowed over a lump in his throat. He knew he was skinny, and he was certain she could see into his soul and know how long it had been since his mom had cooked an actual meal. He kept his gaze lowered, afraid he would cry when she showed him the covered bowl of homemade *miso* soup with healthy chunks of char sui pork, basil and a whole egg. On a plate beside it were two oranges she would have bought when she picked up fresh offerings to be left on the business altar in honor of the gods.

And to his joy, there was a small, fresh, unsliced loaf of peanut butter-flavored bread from a Korean bakery.

Mrs. Wei never overdid her food offerings so as not to embarrass her young employee. He knew that. She left enough that would get him through the night, but not enough to offend Feng's family honor.

"Thank you," he said. None of the food would last very long. He'd really enjoy the meal tonight.

She picked up her things. It was their understanding, and his promise to Mrs. Wei's daughter that his mom would always leave before dark and with him watching her as she got into her car wedged between garbage bins at the back of the building. Hers was the only vehicle allowed back there.

He helped her outside, aware of the strange, heavy mist already rolling over the neighborhood.

"Don't put your brights on," he reminded her. "It will make it harder to see. Please call me when you get home."

He hugged her thin body and he felt her comforting pats on the back.

She gazed at him as she started the engine. She paused, waiting for him to go back inside. He waved from the back door, knowing she hated to leave the front desk unattended, even for these brief moments.

Feng locked and double-bolted the back door, the chill from the mist making him shiver.

Not a creature was stirring back at the front desk, not even their latest nightmare resident, Mrs. Cassidy, who was fond of trooping down to the front desk on an almost hourly basis to complain about everything from loud neighbors to jack-hammers across the street.

He checked the computer for Mrs. Wei's to-do list. Not much, just some filing. She did most of that during the day. He checked the current guest schedule to make sure no late arrivals were due. Two women who were arriving together from Good Luck tours in Shanghai. The good luck was that this company was still in business with their shady dealings. He saw that the women were already late. The company rule was that Feng locked the front doors at ten p.m. owing to the neighborhood. He turned on the outside security cameras to check on people trying to enter the hotel at that time, whether legally or illegally.

A Prime-Time shuttle pulled up. The women came in, bundled in scarves and jackets, wheeling their luggage as if they were carrying unwanted bags of hammers. He'd seen that look before. Shanghai was a long way from here and they'd probably traveled at least eighteen hours.

Feng spoke decent Chinese, a bit of Japanese and even some Korean. He was able to greet the two pretty young women in their own language. He gave them a key to their room, took time to give them a copy of the street map they gave new arrivals. He circled all the places that were still open and could provide them a hot meal.

"Karaoke?" One of them asked.

He smiled. A woman after his own heart. He pointed out the corner block on the map that contained The Shelter Room. The women giggled and thanked him and rolled their stuff toward the elevator. He updated his computer records.

Feng was surprised how many new guests had arrived since he'd left at two a.m. He was relieved at two each morning by a rotating shift of male workers. The owners of the Cedar Hotel tried to keep men only working the front desk after six, owing to the rough neighborhood. Feng had a variety of weapons at his disposal but so far had not needed them. He found himself knocking on his wooden desk as he thought this.

Only Feng and Mrs. Wei worked seven days a week. She started at ten a.m. Or, at least she was supposed to. She usually turned up at nine. She was a true worker.

Six new people had checked in after one o'clock, when Mrs. Wei was left alone until Feng arrived at five. She'd been busy, but then, even when the hotel guests didn't keep her on her feet, she always found some new project around the office to keep her occupied.

Unlike Feng.

He opened his backpack, withdrew the dog-eared copy of *One Piece*, the hottest *manga* to come out of Japan. His best friend, Russell, had lent him the graphic novel and he was enjoying the latest quest of the teenaged hero, Mickey, looking for the One Piece with his ragtag crew that would make him the next pirate king.

Feng reached for the soup. Still warm. He spooned the broth into his mouth and thought about what it would be like to be a pirate king, no worries . . . no casinos . . . his spoon dripped liquid into the bowl. He should check on his father. He didn't want to. One time, he'd called after one of Mom's all-night benders and his mom had answered, irate that she'd woken him. She threatened to come down and *punch his lights out*, but she hadn't. None of his family members ever showed up. Thank God.

Unfortunately, the Chinatown community was small and people talked. It galled him that people felt sorry for Feng and his father. His father should have left her long ago, but his mom's beauty and heartfelt apologies when she was in her right mind kept his dad agog.

He lifted his head after consuming the last bite of egg in the bowl. Checking around to make sure none of their lovely guests were hovering, he opened the *lisee* in his pocket. Sixty dollars. Wow. He could live on that for two weeks. He could buy the *Dragon Ball* and a few cheap meals . . . and, he could even buy back copies of his favorite *manga*.

He removed the cash, put it into his wallet which he kept in a zippered pocket of his jacket and always kept hidden from his mom. The *lisee* he tucked into his journal. He'd hide it in his room. It was way too beautiful to throw away.

"Hey, Feng."

He looked up. Antonio Montoya and his mom, Angie, smiled at him from the counter.

"Are you sure this is okay?" Angie seemed nervous.

"Of course I'm sure," Feng said. He and Mrs. Wei violated a few rules by taking care of little Antonio for three hours whilst his mom took her final subjects at the technical college twice a week. When they went back to their battered women's shelter digs at the end of the week, they missed both Angie and Antonio. They felt they were part of her new secret team helping her shape her new life.

He and Mrs. Wei had already been promised invitations to her farewell party at the refuge when she and Antonio moved into their own permanent housing.

Feng buzzed the door open and Antonio ran in, hugging him. He was a wonderful child, smart, happy, and well-adjusted in spite of his circumstances.

Antonio pulled down his bottom lip. "Look."

The broken, jagged tooth courtesy of a hard slug from his dad had been repaired.

"Fantastic!" Feng said, genuinely pleased.

"I'll be back exactly at nine-thirty," Angie said. A light honk indicated her ride was here. "I'll keep my phone turned on."

"We'll be fine," Feng assured her. Antonio leaned into Feng as they sat behind the counter.

"What are you reading, Feng?"

"One Piece."

The kid shook his head. "I don't know that one. Tell me the story."

Feng smiled and gave him a quick outline, which wasn't easy considering that One Piece was a story that had been published in installments for thirteen years now.

Antonio listed, apparently rapt.

"How about we read it together?" Feng asked.

Antonio nodded.

Feng turned back to page one, happy for an excuse to jump right back into the world of mystical quests and pirate kings. They bent their heads over the *manga* and Feng felt a measure of happiness in the company of a boy, who, like him, didn't expect too much from the real world.

Angie came back right on time as promised and Feng ruffled his little friend's head as Angie took her son back to their room. She always offered Feng money and he always declined.

The elevator pinged and they were gone. The second door opened almost a second later. Feng recognized Xiu Teng, a second-time visitor from China. He'd booked a package deal trip and hated his first assigned room. Feng had given him a better room overlooking the downtown skyline and the young man had been appreciative.

Xiu stepped out of the elevator, hands jammed in his pockets.

"I'm checking out tomorrow. I'm flying back to China," he said, exhaling hard.

Feng nodded. He had no idea why, but this guy seemed attached to the hotel and to the neighborhood. People came to Los Angeles for all kinds of reasons. He had to ask his own father sometime why they moved here from a perfectly nice home in the aptly named Pleasanton up in Northern

California. He still thought about his early childhood romping in snow, among the pines.

"Enjoy your evening, Mr. Teng," he said.

Xiu Teng gave him the ghost of a smile and left the building. Feng's cell phone vibrated. *Dad.*

"Hey, Dad," he said, watching his hotel guest dart across the road between crossing traffic. "How's mom?"

"Still sleeping it off. She's gonna have the mother of all hangovers."

Oh, swell . . .

"Maybe you should, you know . . . um, stay with Russell tonight," his father said. Feng stayed with Russell frequently and was sure it wouldn't be a problem.

"Anything wrong?" he asked, already afraid of the answer.

"She woke up and smashed the place up pretty good. I don't know how much more I can take of this, son."

He didn't respond. His dad said this countless times and always stayed. Feng stayed because he wasn't around nights and when he was there, his mom was usually asleep during the day, same as she was.

"You still there?" Dad asked.

"I'm still here."

"You've got nothing to say?"

"Nope. Not really. Got a new guest, Dad." He ended the call. Sooner rather than later, Feng would give up on both of them and walk away from them. Forever.

Feng left the hotel a little after two, relieved by a new guy, Jimmy. He was kinda jumpy, but then two a.m. was a weird time for anybody to start their work shift. He'd come armed with a thermos of coffee and said he'd just woken from a deep sleep, which explained his edginess.

He checked up and down the street, the sixty bucks in his wallet burning a hole into his zippered pocket. Feng made a quick left, walking right into the shadowy mist. He heard no voices. He knew how to walk into J-Town avoiding Skid Row and any potential danger. He zeroed in on the small, lively, neon lit First Street strip mall that took up the entire corner. It was jumping, even at this hour. Even the cafés and grocery stores were packed.

Feng moved through the dark fog, picking out faces he knew from the long line of people waiting on the stairs to get into the Shelter Room on the second floor. Music pumped out of it, making his heart pound in a crazy-good way. He'd just reached the ground floor terrace, energized by the great vibe of the mall.

"Hi! Feng!"

He was stunned to see Ki, the object of his affection, waving to him from the top of the steps. People hung back, letting Feng pass. It seemed like a misty night miracle when Ki clasped his shoulder and said,

"Let's sing a duet!"

He paid his five-dollar entry fee and left his backpack on the side of the stage with the transvestite DJ, Half Dolly, who watched your stuff if you bought her beers.

Feng felt the applause of the crowd warming him, adding to the shocking revelation that Ki actually knew his name.

"And now, ladies and gentlemen," Half Dolly said, joining them onstage in a dazzling pink and white polka dot fifties style, puffy dress, "our fave twinks, Feng and Ki, singing, what else . . . Lady Gaga!"

Feng felt a moment of panic but took the mike from Ki and they began to sing. They plowed through two Gaga numbers and Feng felt Ki's hand on his shoulder as he read off the lyrics from the screen on the wall and sang his guts out.

"Let's get a drink," Ki said as they took their bows.

They jumped from the stage to raucous applause and blinding strobes. Feng reached for his backpack and felt Ki tugging him toward the bar. He thought he might die from happiness. At the bar, they each bought a Sapporo and Feng bought one for the DJ, muscling through the throng to give Half Dolly her drink.

She flapped long eyelashes at him, blowing him a cherry-red kiss. He laughed. It was turning into a great night. Ki tugged him again and they pushed their way out of the club and to the back terrace, where the chilly drop in temperature after the warm crush of bodies inside the club felt great. Through the thick haze of fog, Feng glimpsed Russell, who was leaning against the railing, chatting up a guy Feng knew his friend had been chasing for months now.

"Hey," Feng said, aware of Ki's presence beside him. "Can I crash at your place tonight?"

"Sure," Russell said. He winked at Feng. "You got the key, right?"

Feng nodded. As Russell and his friend moved on to a more private patch on the balcony, Russell grabbed Feng's arm.

"Let's hope I'm not there when you arrive. I might get lucky tonight."

Feng grinned. "You'll get lucky, I just know it."

Ki touched Feng's shoulder. "Look at the fucking mist, man, can you believe it?"

From up here, it was a startling sight. It resembled a gigantic gray-black cloak hovering between the earth and sky. Almost like a pair of —

"It kind of looks like wings, doesn't it?" Ki asked, taking a long pull at his beer.

Feng glanced at him. Why were they out here? It wasn't that he hadn't pined for time and attention from this guy, but it was so out of character. Feng could hear the low moans around them. They'd all come out here for the anonymity, the safety of the dark mist.

Ki pulled Feng into a dark corner of the building as another couple vacated it. Feng could still feel the warmth of the last guy's body on the brick wall. He was astonished when Ki pressed into him, kissing him. He returned the man's kisses, tasting the tang of cold beer on his tongue.

Feng gave himself up to the soft lips probing his. The kiss deepened, Ki sighing into Feng's mouth as their tongues met. Ki's free hand slipped behind Feng's head, cupping it lightly. Ki stopped kissing him, waiting for Feng to do the work. Feng kept kissing Ki, sucking his tongue. Ki pressed into him, Feng feeling the man's cock hardening against his belly. It was the most erotic moment of Feng's life.

Ki withdrew from him, keeping contact only from the groin. In the deep darkness, Feng could feel the man's hot stare on his face. The swirl of lights from inside the club and shone briefly on Ki's face. He took another swig of his beer and smiled at Feng. He leaned in again, letting the beer seep into Feng's mouth. Feng sucked it all down as Ki rubbed against him.

Feng knew then. Ki wanted Feng to suck his cock. Ki took Feng's beer out of his hand and kissed him again. Feng fumbled at the zipper of Ki's jeans. He slid down the wall and reached into the surprisingly colorful underpants Ki wore, for his cock. It was slim, but very, very long and leaped at him like a snake disturbed from slumber. Feng hooked one finger over the base, licked at the head and then, began to suck. He was aware of the voices then, the increasing sounds of sucking and fucking around him.

"Hurry," Ki said, "we gotta sing again."

We. Feng put all his efforts to giving the guy a monster blowjob, Ki gently fucking his face. Feng took as much of the cock as he could into his mouth, Ki increasing his thrusts. He was close. Feng could taste the pre-come, felt it coating his throat. He heard Ki moaning.

"Yeah, Feng, yeah, like that. Just like that."

Feng grasped the man's balls for an extra surge of bliss to his now-panting recipient. He was in a zone with Ki's cock. He wished he could prolong the experience for himself, but was completely submerged in Feng's mouth, and his body started to shake.

Banpaia!

Feng's eyes flew open. Who had said that? Nobody else was close, as far as he could tell, but the voice had whispered right in his ear. Feng kept sucking as Ki gave one last, quick thrust.

Ki came, Feng released him, and Ki pulled back. He helped Feng to his feet. Feng was pleased to see the shocked expression in the other man's eyes.

"Wow," Ki said. "That was amazing."

He handed the bottles to Feng as he zipped himself back into his pants.

Ki kissed him. Feng put the heavier of the two bottles to his lips and drank.

"I'll return the favor next time," Ki said, smiling and running his hand alone Feng's straining cock, still trapped in his pants.

Feng nodded. He didn't care about next time. He was happy for now. They made it back into the club, Half Dolly pretending to be cranky with them.

"And here they are, our two favorite twinkbirds, ladies and gentlemen," she crooned into the mike. "And what are you going to sing for us?" she asked, holding the mike to Ki's face.

Ki squeezed Feng's hand and said, "*Bad Romance*," making Feng laugh.

CHAPTER TWO

H e slipped into Russell's loft apartment a little after six o'clock in the morning. Russell's apartment was on the third floor of a warehouse in the center of Chinatown's marketplace on Hill Street, in the heart of the historic neighborhood.

Russell wasn't around, but damp towels on the bathroom floor and a swirl of mist still evaporating in it indicated a recent hot shower.

Feng liked the place. It was very small. Its single bedroom was big enough for a double bed and not much else. The kitchen reminded him of a ship's galley, long and narrow. The living room contained a sofa, a wing chair and a small dining table Russell had bought from a Japanese catalogue. Japanese companies specialized in furnishing small spaces. Feng coveted the space and was grateful to have a friend who didn't mind sharing it with him when the need arose.

His cell phone vibrated. A text from Ki. *See you tonight.* He smiled to himself. It was four days before Halloween. Still hard to believe his luck with Ki. It had been the best night of his life and he still had tonight to look forward to.

They had agreed to text each other that they were home safe. Rumors had swirled in the club that another guy had disappeared.

He quickly texted back. *Had so much fun. Can't wait.* He lay on Russell's damned uncomfortable, geometric sofa the family that owned the gigantic furniture store downstairs had talked him into. He squirmed until he was sort of comfortable.

18

His legs were too long and dangled over the arm of the sofa. He felt his vertebrae falling into place. Oddly, the sofa put his back into alignment each and every time. It just wasn't a very pleasant sensation. Torn between sleep and wanting a cup of coffee so he could savor the memory of the last few hours, he realized he couldn't move. He dozed on and off, not moving much until he heard a key in the door. He sat up, still drowsy and saw that it was Russell.

"Hey, you," his friend said.

"Hey, yourself. Did you get lucky?"

Russell gave him a twisted grin. "Yeah, lucky they still had donuts over at Ling's." He held up a greasy bag.

"Your guy's still holding out on you?"

Russell shrugged. "We kissed a little. He was spooked when all the talk started about yet another guy vanishing. What do you make of it all?"

Feng shook his head. "I don't know, to be honest, but that fog is so weird, isn't it?"

Russell dropped the donut bag on his tiny dining room table and glanced out the window.

"I'll say. It's kind of . . . ominous. During the day, you can sort of convince yourself it isn't real . . . but seventeen guys . . . that's real enough."

He peeled off his leather jacket and threw it across a chair.

"Have you watched CNN? What do they say?"

Feng shook his head. "Nah . . . I was trying to catch some zzz's."

Russell picked up his remote and his giant, flat-screen TV came to life. He flicked through channels and left the TV on CNN.

Feng forced himself off the sofa as Russell put the kettle on the stove. Russell seemed a little down. Probably not a good time for Feng to tell him he'd gotten frisky with Ki.

Russell was a handsome Chinese guy, two years older than

Feng and making pretty good money as an IT supervisor for a major software company. He worked crazy-long hours and what little free time he had, like Feng, he loved the karaoke bar in J-Town.

Feng opened his backpack and removed the copy of *One Piece* that his friend had lent him. He couldn't wait to check out the magazine stand at the grocery store downstairs and pick up the latest *Dragon Ball*.

"What did you think?" Russell asked him.

"It was cool." He shook his head. "The artist is pretty amazing, especially now they've stepped up production releasing so many novels a month."

"I know, right?"

Russell poured their coffee and they dunked their donuts in companionable silence. Russell could afford to buy not only the *manga* novels, but the DVDs as well. He lent Feng a few of his recent ones and they spent a good hour poring through the latest Japanese *manga* he'd purchased, Russell insisting that Feng borrow a couple of other stories, too. Their shared passion for myth and story had cemented their friendship, which began in middle school. In those days, they spent hours creating mixed tapes of their favorite songs. Now they obsessed over *anime*. Feng never stopped feeling grateful that now that Russell was a successful businessman and Feng skirted the fringes of their shared dreams to become film directors and writers, nothing had changed.

"How's your mom?" Russell asked.

"The same."

Feng licked sugar from his fingertips. In spite of their shared passions, they couldn't have been more different in some ways. Russell was what was known as a *Parachute Kid*. His parents had brought him and his sister to Los Angeles as pre-teens, setting them up in the posh suburb of San Marino, now almost entirely populated by other Asian *Parachute Kids*.

Like Russell, these kids were abandoned by their wealthy parents who left their children to their own devices, with a boatload of money to support them. Russell had done well and was a credit to his family back in Hong Kong. His sister had gone off the rails getting into a teen gang, but was now carving a niche for herself as a model in London.

No matter how bad Feng's mom got with her drinking, there were times when she was sweet, and she was *there*. His dad, when he was working, had been fun and full of life. Dad would get a job again . . . he had to.

Russell took the cups into the kitchen and waved off Feng's attempts to wash them. He stacked them in the dishwasher.

"Sleep on my bed," he offered. "I have to get to work."

Feng was in no shape to argue. He heard the front door close with a soft click as he lay on Russell's bed. The next time he opened his eyes, it was four o'clock in the afternoon. He couldn't believe he'd slept so long.

He took a shower, glad that he kept a change of underwear and a clean T-shirt as well as his toothbrush in his backpack.

He checked the newspaper section of the catch-all grocery store downstairs. Not a single issue of *Dragon Ball* or *One Piece* left.

"Just sold the last one," the storekeeper told him. "Sorry about that."

He checked his watch. If he grabbed the number fourteen bus, he could make it to J-Town and check the store on the corner. The bus pulled up, making Feng feel like it was his lucky day. He greeted the driver, paid his fare and took a seat near the front. In this neighborhood, all the troublemakers sat in back. He silently cursed every red light they hit until they arrived in J-Town. He thanked the driver, covering the last few blocks on foot.

Once again, neither of the graphic novels was there, but Feng was astonished to see a brand new graphic novel, at least it was new to him. It was called *Banpaia*. It was thick and heavy, the cover a glossy black with gray wings embossed on it in an almost velvety material. The wings made him think of the night mist. He longed to know who the artist was, but he didn't have to time to check the contents.

"How much?" he asked the storekeeper, pleased and surprised to find it was only two dollars. It was thick and heavy and big, about eleven inches long. He badly wanted to call Russell and report his find, but he was already running late. He paid for his novel and tore down the street, making it to the Cedar House with seconds to spare for his evening shift.

Feng walked in, surprised when Mrs. Wei didn't greet him at the front desk. Right away, he knew something was wrong. The door that they always kept locked between the public and staff, was cracked open. *Holy shit.*

He smelled something funny. A strange metallic smell. Opening the door, fear washed over him, but he knew he had to go into the front office. And there she was, lying on the floor, a great, big, butcher's knife sticking out of her chest.

Feng knew she was dead.

Her sightless eyes stared up, her mouth open in an expression of agony, as if her last moments on Earth had been filled with terror and pain.

"Mrs. Wei?"

It was useless. He knew it was too late. How long had she laid here? He saw her purse sprawled on the floor, the contents tossed. The scene was frenzied. Almost too frenzied. He didn't want to touch anything more than he had. He stood, feeling dizzy and called 911.

Feng stood, watching over the kindest woman he'd known, wondering who would do this to her. He was still in shock when the police arrived to ask their endless damned questions. Their voices came to him, in and out, like a radio frequency that didn't quite work. Somebody took him outside, where he sat on the pavement and cried.

Mrs. Wei was quite a fixture in the neighborhood. He'd been unable to act beyond calling the cops. The coroner's office came, detectives, too. Somebody called her daughter, who arrived and sat out front with Feng, crying too.

Feng wondered who would do something like this to Mrs. Wei. Who could hate her enough? The local news crews found out about the murder. He could hear the blonde, pretty reporter from Channel Three, beating the story up into a frenzied, bloody sensation. Another senseless killing in the seedy heart of downtown LA.

"Hot on the heels of the seventeenth young man to disappear from this neighborhood comes news that an elderly hotel manager has been brutally killed," she said. Feng felt himself tuning into his surroundings at that moment.

"Come with me," said a guy who flashed a detective's badge and took him to an unmarked vehicle. He put Feng in the passenger seat and sat beside him.

Feng had already answered the same questions over and over. He'd just arrived, he'd already said. Same time as always. He'd realized something was off because the door to the office was open. Mrs. Wei never left it open.

"Any of the guests have a beef with her?" the detective asked.

Feng tried to think.

"We're not the Biltmore," he said, gesturing to the tall building up on the hill above them, the swanky part of downtown. "People get funny notions, like they should have a bigger, better room. We always try to accommodate them."

"Any of these names familiar to you?" The detective slid a piece of paper toward him.

"Yeah. Wait. This one is new. Did he check in today?"

"No idea," the detective said. "His name is on the register, but he has no room number." He asked Feng a few more questions.

"Where will you be if we need to speak to you?" the cop asked.

"You mean I won't be working tonight?"

"Not yet. We'll be processing the lobby area, dusting for prints. We'll need yours for comparison."

Feng nodded. None of this felt real.

"You're really in shock," the detective said.

"Of course I am. She's a wonderful woman. She's so good to me."

The detective nodded.

"I'm sorry for your loss."

He got out of the car and Feng watched the cop walk around the vehicle, not sure if he was supposed to get out, too. The cop beckoned him, and Feng got out, aware of the crush of onlookers. He noticed a couple of Ki's buddies, but Ki wasn't there.

Feng followed the detective into a mobile unit where Feng gave them his California ID card and submitted his prints. The cop kept asking questions.

"What time does your shift normally end?"

"Two a.m."

"Weird hours for a kid."

"It's a job. And I'm twenty-one."

The detective said nothing.

"You want a cup of tea?" a female officer asked him.

Feng nodded and she poured some from a thermos into a paper cup. It was hot and sweet and he felt his hands shaking as he tried to sip it. He tried to relax and it started to work, even as he looked out at the growing throng around the yellow crime scene tape. Mrs. Wei's daughter had starting crying and screaming again. Her mother's body made its last trip out of the hotel. Feng thought it was ironic that it was via the front door.

"Is her car out the back?" he asked no-one in particular. The female officer radioed for the detective, who returned.

"She always drove home. It was part of my job to make sure she got into her car, that it started and she was on her way," he said.

"No car," the cop said. "You know the make and model?"

"A white Ford Taurus. It's a 2003."

"You happen to know the license number?"

Feng thought a moment. "First three letters are HSN. Sorry . . . I can't remember the numbers." He paused. "She just renewed her car insurance and upgraded it. There should be a folder on her desk with the information. I filed it myself two days ago."

The detective nodded.

"How do you get to and from work?"

"Bus, train, and on foot."

"What were you doing before you arrived this evening?"

Feng felt a shiver crawl up his spine. The strange mist had started encroaching across the sky, but it wasn't that. He'd answered the same questions over and over. He repeated everything.

"We've been unable to verify your account with Russell Chang," the detective said. "We called his office and his cellphone. Apparently, he never showed up to work this morning."

Feng stared at the cop.

"What are you suggesting? That I had something to do with this?"

"No. We're saying we can't establish your alibi."

"My *alibi?*" What was the guy talking about? "Detective . . ."

"Stevens."

"Stevens. I worked until two a.m. I went to the karaoke bar. I did everything I told you I did. A guy called Jimmy relieved me at two. He's new. Worked a couple of nights now. If there was a problem after I left, I wouldn't know about it unless Mrs. Wei called me and told me, and she didn't do that. After Jimmy leaves, she's on her own for a few hours and I come in at five."

The detective said nothing for a moment.

"Can anyone verify seeing you between four and five?"

"Is that when . . . you know?"

"Detective Stevens nodded.

"I took the bus and I walked. I woke up late. I woke up at four o'clock and I raced to get here." He tried to digest everything he'd just heard. The news about Russell not being at work was weird.

"Russell didn't make it to work? That's crazy. He left his apartment right at seven. We had coffee and donuts together."

Feng started to worry. He'd felt so good that morning . . . now his life was shot to shit. Mrs. Wei was dead, Russell was missing.

"Write down for me the bus number you took, the route you walked," Stevens said. "I'd also like your permission to go into Russell's apartment. Do you have a key?"

Feng nodded. He dug into his backpack and handed over the key. He realized in that moment that the graphic novel of *Banpaia* was gone. He was certain he put it in his backpack when he paid for it. Maybe he'd forgotten it in his haste.

"Why don't you come with me?" Stevens asked. "By the time we're done, you can probably get back to work."

"Okay," Feng said. He had a spooky feeling the key part had been a test, that maybe the cop would have pressed him more had he declined to hand it over.

"Do you mind if I try texting Russell?" Feng asked. "This isn't like him. He loves his job. He always leaves nice and early to get there." He stopped talking.

"What?" the detective prompted.

"I was just thinking. He's a true worker. Just like Mrs. Wei."

"Knock yourself out," Stevens said. "Go ahead and call him."

Considering he'd just found Mrs. Wei on the floor dead, the cop's words seemed cruel and offhand to Feng. He said nothing though as Feng sent a text to his friend. As they drove toward Chinatown, he tried to leave him a message, but Russell's voicemail box was full.

Feng knew then that Russell was in trouble.

He was back behind the front desk at ten p.m. watching the evening news. The murder of Mrs. Wei overshadowed the news of Russell's disappearance, but the media was already claiming him as vanished victim number eighteen.

Feng swallowed over the lump in his throat. He opened his backpack and was surprise to find *Banpaia* was there after all. *What the . . .*

Feng opened the first page, liking the feel of the paper and the artwork. The artist's name was unfamiliar to him, but the man's work was incredible.

Banpaia, he learned, was a centuries-old vampire who came to big cities where there was trouble and stole away the handsome young men in the middle of the night.

No . . . it couldn't be . . . He kept reading. The vampire seduced the men physically, emotionally, and spiritually. All lacked something in their lives that he promised them.

Some had forgotten their dreams, some lived with prolonged abuse.

Feng felt his mouth go dry.

How had an artist in Tokyo come up with such a concept?

Holy moly . . . the strange mist is in the story!

Frame after frame showed the dark, hovering image above the dialogue bubbles.

Feng stared at the page he'd just turned. The man in the image looked eerily like Russell. Nah, he was imagining things.

He stared at *Banpaia*, a handsome, reed-slim man whose thin built belied a fantastic body that was well-muscled. Oh, he was handsome. His jet-black hair and black eyes beguiled him from the page. He seemed very, very real. The hint of fangs was sexy . . . deadly.

The office phone rang. Feng jumped. He answered it.

"Good evening, Cedar House hotel. May I help you?"

Silence, then a click.

Feng shivered. It was creepy and spooky sitting right near where Mrs. Wei had been killed, but the owners had demanded that the hotel remain operational. Two detectives had swirled around Feng as he handled the emergency checkouts. They were now down several guests. Some of them had checked out in fright and he couldn't blame them. Poor Angie Montoya had waited until Feng was on his own and had done a moonlight flit with Antonio, petrified that her husband would catch a glimpse of her on the evening news. Feng had called the battered women's shelter where she stayed most of the time and he was pleased when one of the nuns arrived at the back door to collect her.

She didn't tell Feng where she was taking Angie and Antonio and he didn't ask. It was safer for Angie that way. He had a peculiar feeling as he watched the nun driving away that he would never see Angie again and he shrugged off the notion.

He'd texted Ki, but got no response. Depression sank into his skin, heavier than the damned mist. Detective Stevens came in shortly before midnight with more questions and more veiled innuendo. Luckily, Feng had used Russell's phone around four-fifteen to call his dad when he'd realized his cell phone battery was flat. He and Russell had the exact same phones, so he'd borrowed one of Russell's charged batteries.

The cops had checked the phone records, and according to the detective, the bus driver had verified that Feng had taken the four-twenty-five bus into J-Town. Stevens seemed almost disappointed when he reported that almost everybody had told him how close Feng and Mrs. Wei had been.

"Almost?" Feng said.

"One of the guests said she picks on you a bit."

"She has sciatica. It plays up sometimes. She's the kindest woman I know."

Stevens didn't respond. He poked around the office for a moment and then said he wanted to interview the housekeeping staff. Somebody had asked Feng about this earlier, but they'd been throwing questions at him all afternoon like hand grenades. He forgot who asked him what.

"It's not your fault," Stevens said, his voice sounding kind. "I can see this has been a shock and nobody else was around to get the list from. Our priority was processing the room."

"She's never going to come in here and give me half her dinner again."

The realization hit Feng like a punch to the chest and tears wallowed in his eyes. God, it was hopeless.

Stevens patted his shoulder as Feng cried.

"I'm sorry," Feng said, trying hard to pull himself together.

Stevens shrugged. "It's hard to find a dead body, Feng. You manned up today."

Manned up. Feng felt like shit. He reached for a tissue from the box on Mrs. Wei's desk. It was covered in Chinese fan paper. She loved little, pretty things.

"Any news on Russell?" he asked.

Stevens shook his head. He took a seat on the other side of the desk, where Feng usually sat and talked with Mrs. Wei. She would never sit in this chair again. He braced himself against another emotional surge.

He gave Stevens a hard copy containing the names and addresses of the current housekeeping employees.

"There are five of them and they all get in at six a.m. You can check with Jimmy about which ones turned up today, but he hasn't left a note that I can see indicating there was a problem."

"What about room service?"

Room service? Feng almost laughed.

"No," he said. "We don't provide meals."

"Was there a problem with any of the guests this week?"

"Not enough to kill Mrs. Wei, if that's what you're asking."

"No. I'm asking you if there was a problem with any guest this week."

Feng glanced away from the cop, then opened his backpack.

"I kept a list. I always do."

Stevens leaned against the hardback chair as Feng reeled off the list of complaints from various guests. He'd noted the dates, times, the complainant, the nature of the complaint and the outcome. Stevens looked astonished.

"So . . . this Mrs. Cassidy complains . . . a lot?"

"Every day."

"Can I have a copy of your report?"

"It's okay for me to use the photocopier, right?"

"Right. We're done in here. We covered the room."

Feng ran off a copy and handed it to Stevens.

"Do you keep an official record on the computer as well?" Stevens asked.

"No."

"No? Why not?"

Feng hesitated. "I . . . look . . . Mrs. Wei is an incredibly nice lady. Some of the people here are down on their luck and she tries to help them. Sometimes . . . and she's not supposed to, ok? But sometimes she lets them use the computer to email a resume or check on job interviews. We have locked files on the computer for bills and customer receipts, but we also keep paper copies, too. The report I gave you is kept by me and Mrs. Wei has one, too. We don't keep things that might upset the clients on the computer. We had that mistake happen one time."

"Who was it with? Can you remember?"

"Yes, I can, actually. He's on your list. A Chinese tourist named Xiu Teng."

"What happened?"

Feng thought back to the horrible moment that he and Mrs. Wei had caught Teng scrolling through the complaints he'd found on the computer, mocking them.

"You think I'm difficult?" he'd yelled.

Feng described how they gave him a free night's accommodation, but he hadn't been happy at all with the hotel, or his room.

"This is his second visit and both times he's clashed with Mrs. Wei about his room. This time, I gave him a new room when I came on shift."

"What about the first time?"

Feng shrugged. "We were full, and he wasn't happy. I was surprised when he showed up again."

"Which room is he in?"

"He checked out today. He told me last night he was going home to China. He didn't seem very happy about that."

Stevens thanked him and left the hotel. Feng locked up behind him, barely able to see the detective as the thicker-than-ever mist folded in on him as Stevens got into his car.

Feng wondered why he watched as Stevens drove off and realized it was habit.

He's a big, bad cop. He can take care of himself.

His cell phone vibrated in his pocket. It was a text from his

31

father.

He checked the readout: *Don't come home.*

Feng gaped at it. Was his dad serious?

He put a quick call through to him.

His father answered on a whisper. "The police have been here asking questions about you."

"Me? But I've done nothing wrong!"

"Feng, they've been in touch with the casino. They knew your mom owed them a lot of money. They say money went missing from the hotel. They think you stole it to cover her debt!"

"That's ridiculous," Feng said. "One of the detectives was just here. He said nothing about there being any missing money."

"Feng, just stay away."

His father hung up and Feng stared off into space. None of this made any sense. He heard a knock at the front desk. One of the guests was complaining about the ice machine being broken on the fourth floor.

It had been broken for days. Feng gave the woman a tray of ice from the staff fridge.

"Thanks," she said. "I'll bring it back down in the morning."

Feng had a busy night. Stevens came back before two and Feng was amazed the guy still seemed full of stamina.

"I want to interview Jimmy," Stevens said. "He should be here soon, right?"

"Right."

"We haven't been able to reach him. The numbers and address you have for him are invalid. The address is a vacant lot."

Feng stared at him.

"My parents tell me you think I killed Mrs. Wei for her

money."

Stevens looked startled. He threw up his hands and shook his head.

"Look, this case just started, and we jumped in not knowing too much about Mrs. Wei. Or you. We've checked into your family background. I know your mom has a severe gambling problem and your father admitted you're supporting them. I saw footage of you going to casino and vouching for your mother never going in there again. You seem like a nice, bright kid who's working long hours."

He paused.

"The hotel owner claims a significant amount of money was stolen here today but I can't get any verification. He's coming down from San Francisco and should be here in the morning. Mrs. Wei's daughter says this type of claim is typical of the owner. She doesn't think there was ever a huge amount of money left here."

Feng nodded. "She's right."

"All your accounting here is up to date. I asked your parents a couple of questions. I think it's pretty rough that they jumped to conclusions."

"My dad told me not to come home. He sent me a text."

Stevens didn't respond. What could he say?

I'm homeless. Hot damn. And after this horrible day I'll probably be out of a job.

He sat and waited for Jimmy in silence with the cop who scrolled through his messages on his cell phone. Jimmy was very late now, and Feng started to worry.

"What if he's disappeared?" Feng asked. Jimmy wasn't that cute but heck, guys were disappearing around town faster than Feng could keep track of them.

Stevens said nothing.

Feng was relieved when, at two thirty-two in the morning, Jimmy knocked on the front door of the hotel.

"That him?" Stevens asked.

Feng nodded.

"Don't bother letting him in."

Feng watched on the closed circuit TV as the security camera caught the image of Jimmy being wrestled to the ground by two uniformed officers.

He screamed and yelled. Feng heard a lot of cussing and stared in shock as Jimmy kicked out at the officers. They dragged him away.

Feng saw another image appearing under the camera. It was the owner. Feng blew out a sigh. He knew, just knew that it would be bad news.

"I'm sorry," Mr. Huang said, as Feng opened the door. "But I'm going to have to let you go."

CHAPTER THREE

There had been no word from Ki. Feng dreaded getting to the Shelter Room and finding he was with someone else. The news was even worse. Ki was missing. Feng stumbled joining the waiting lineup on the stairs, listening to the chatter.

And then he ran into somebody who pointed to a guy saying, "Vincent disappeared, but he's back. He can't say where he's been. Bet he was taking drugs."

Feng looked, but couldn't see much in the thick fog. He waited with all the other people to get into the club but when he got inside, the news was no better. Half Dolly had no news. She sipped her beer through a straw.

"I just got botox, darling. Face is fucking frozen. But if I could move a muscle, you'd see I was sad. Very sad. Ki's one of my favorites."

He moved through the crowd. The mood was strange. People were nervous. He noticed one guy sniffing his drink as if suspecting somebody had slipped him drugs. Feng felt removed from it all. And then he noticed people shrinking away from him.

"That's the guy that killed the old lady," he heard somebody saying as soon as there was a pause in the music.

"We don't want killers here!" a guy shouted, throwing his drink in Feng's face. Spirits. He smelled whisky and it stung his eyes, blinding him. People threw things at him. A bottle hit his head. He fell to the ground, blood streaming from his scalp, he felt strong hands dragging him. He fought off the

35

attack, but it wasn't an attack, it was Half Dolly pulling him to safety. She got him to the front door.

"Run!" she screamed.

And he did.

He lost his pursuers, thankful for the thick, blanketing haze which became his friend. He ran until he no longer heard footsteps or the jeering voices. He shrank against a cold, stone wall taking big, gulping breaths. He was tired, hungry, and alone. He was tired of this life. Of things never going right for him. He was tired of being tired. But now he was also scared. People wanted to frame him for Mrs. Wei's murder. He heard the rush of a train and realized that in the mist, he'd lost his way and had stumbled into the railway tracks of the Blue Line.

Feng paused, watching east and west-bound trains passing each other across the vast expanse of metal tracks. He could wait and hurl himself in front of the next one coming. He should take the west-bound train, which dipped south, ending in Disneyland. He hadn't been to Disneyland once since his family had moved here and it was only fifty minutes away by car.

He started crossing over the tracks, seeing the downtown city skyline through the haze. Staples Center, Philippe the Original . . . too bad he wouldn't get a decent French dip sandwich before he died. He was so hungry. Soooo hungry. He could feel the rustle of movement on the track beneath his foot. The train was coming from behind him. He checked up and down the platform. It was heading east. Oh, too bad. Maybe he never was meant to get to Disneyland.

Should he jump, stand on the track with his eyes closed or lay across the tracks? He had to decide quickly. His terror mounted. He wasn't afraid to die. He was afraid he'd survive, mangled in a heap of muscle and bone.

Don't come home.

Old lady killer.

The train was coming. He felt the rush of wind. The lights almost blinded him as he set a trembling foot on the track.

Stand here and close your eyes. Don't look.

The train's warning siren blared. He caught a glimpse of something . . . someone ahead of him.

Was it an angel?

He blinked.

Banpaia.

The black angel soared, rose, came straight toward him. The angel snatched him away from the blare of the train's progress.

Feng fell to the ground, hard, across a train track, his entire body aching. The train rushed by, a rocket of heat and glare. He laid there, a single fat tear trickling from his eye, into his ear.

No angel. He'd chickened out.

How the fuck?? I was ready to die. Shit!

How long until the next one?

He gathered his wits. Sat up. And saw him. The vampire was crouched beside him. He knew it was him.

"It's you, isn't it?" Feng asked, bewildered . . . mesmerized.

The man stared down at him. He extended a hand to Feng.

"You belong to me now."

Through the chilly, snapping mist, they walked, hand in hand. Feng kept staring at the man. It was him, he knew it was him, but how? He felt as if he'd disappeared into his own *manga* . . . his own private world of heroes and shape shifters. Maybe he was already dead?

The vampire turned and smiled.

"You are very much alive, Feng. I need you that way."

They walked together, a long, long walk that could not have been more beautiful for Feng. The vampire played with his fingers, kissing each one. They stopped on a desolate downtown corner, one of his favorites, because it always looked like New York to Feng. The vampire kissed Feng's thumb, his mouth moving up his hand, turning it, his lips pressing to Feng's soft, milky wrist.

Feng could feel his own heartbeat pounding in his chest. The vampire moved upward to Feng's inner elbow, kissing crevices that Feng never knew could ignite erotic desire in him. The lights turned green.

The vampire stopped kissing him, but still held his hand. Feng felt as if he were on the verge of coming and *Banpaia* hadn't even kissed his mouth yet.

Banpaia pressed him up against a wall of an office building, his mouth close, oh, so close, then he took his face away again, Feng trembling with the sensation of almost-bliss.

They walked toward Chinatown. Feng could smell the lingering scent of barbecued meats still strong on the air. Feng looked up and saw his favorite familiar sight from his bedroom; the red lanterns dangling above the main street. His glance shot straight across to his parents' apartment. A single light was on. His room. He had the noisiest room overlooking Hill Street. Why was his light on?

Suddenly, he didn't care. His life with his parents seemed like a thousand years ago.

Don't come home.

It wasn't his home . . . or his problem anymore.

He and *Banpaia* walked to Russell's building. How did the vampire know where it was? How did he know anything? They entered Russell's apartment. Feng reached for the light switch in the living room, but the vampire held his hand back. He leaned over, opening a window in the living room, smiling at Feng. In the muted, crimson light from the red lanterns dancing high in the marketplace, Feng saw desire and need flare in the other man's eyes.

"Kiss me," *Banpaia* said.

In the darkness, dusted by tendrils of mist, Feng let the vampire undress him. He took his time. He explored each new inch of Feng's exposed skin as one might pause with delight over an exquisite piece of pottery exposed from careful tissue wrapping. Feng felt both fragile and beautiful under the vampire's feather touch.

When *Banpaia* kissed him at last, for the first time in his life, he felt loved.

They went to the bedroom, Feng hardly able to believe they were together. *Banpaia's* seduction never hastened. He put Feng on the bed on his back and stroked his feet and legs, moving up Feng's body, taking Feng's cock into his long fingers. Feng knew that for an Asian man, he was pretty well endowed. He didn't make a big deal of it. He usually suffered his relentless horniness in silence. Still fully clothed, *Banpaia* bent his head and sucked Feng to an orgasm. He stood, his gaze never leaving Feng's cock, which still stood, hard, needy, as the vampire undid his black shirt.

Feng kept his half-open eyes open so he could see the vampire's loveliness. He was surprised that the black shirt and pants seemed to be one. They fell away leaving a black leather codpiece. Feng longed to put his face to it, to inhale the vampire's scent.

Banpaia strode to him then, the codpiece vanishing and leaving an incredibly thick, long cock that hardened the second Feng touched it. *Banpaia* stood at the side of the bed, allowing Feng to suck him. He made sounds, lovely, appreciative sounds deep in his throat as Feng gave the vampire the best blowjob he'd ever given a man. The vampire licked his fingertips and leaned down, tracing Feng's left nipple. Feng felt the sensation of erotic flush shoot straight to his cock. He sucked, enjoying the flavor of the vampire's beautiful cock, but then *Banpaia* pulled away.

He got on the bed, pushing Feng's legs back. He rubbed his now-slick cockhead against Feng's ass. It had been so long since Feng had been fucked and he wanted it. Badly. The vampire held Feng's legs apart, as if he enjoyed watching his cock do divine things to Feng's body. They had no rubbers . . . *wait do vampires use rubbers?* Feng wondered, catching his breath.

Feng was always amazed how one little place on a man's body could generate such rhythm of fire. His entire body shuddered with each thrust and parry from the vampire's massive cock.

Finally his cockhead slipped inside Feng's tight opening.

Feng realized he was begging and began to babble. He wanted the vampire in him.

Banpaia leaned down, Feng caught the flash of elongated teeth as they bit into Feng's neck.

Feng came a second time before the man was even fully in him. He clutched the vampire's smooth ass cheeks with sweaty hands. *Banpaia's* teeth left Feng's neck, a tiny dot of blood at the corner of his lip.

"Tell me," he said. "Tell me what I want to hear."

"I'm yours," Feng said.

The vampire's eyes glowed as his cock submerged itself inside Feng completely. Feng was astonished to come a third time, even deeper, harder than the first time.

Banpaia bit into his neck again and Feng cried out in sheer pleasure.

Feng awoke in the morning, the shouts of early morning activity floating up to him. He turned and checked. *Banpaia* was gone. Milk deliveries, bread deliveries . . . running feet. Somebody coughing. He heard it all. It was deafening. He raised himself from the bed, feeling languid. *Banpaia* had fucked and sucked on him for hours. Feng stepped into the bathroom and checked his throat, surprised to see the two puncture points he felt certain would be there, were not. Nothing. He stared harder.

Not even a slight bruise.

He felt as if it could have been a dream except that he hadn't been fucked in such a long time and his ass hurt a little now that he was up and moving. It hurt so good. He didn't want to shower and wash off the vampire's body. He caught a mental flash of the vampire's mouth roaming him.

Or his kisses.

He tried to pee, but couldn't.

Coffee. He wanted coffee. He stood at the kitchen door, staring into the empty room and the bamboo plant Russell had put on the sill for good luck.

Where was he? Was he okay?

He couldn't be here in daylight without his friend. It felt too sad. He'd get coffee outside. Feng slipped into his clothes and shoes, picked up his backpack and went downstairs.

People rushed by him and he greeted them. Nobody responded. Well, it was early. They were busy. He thought about what he would do with his time now that he was a free agent. He finally allowed himself to think a little bit about getting the sack from his boss last night. It really grilled his cheese knowing that his boss at the Cedar House had given him a check with slightly more than a full week's pay in it. He'd written final wages in the memo section at the bottom. Feng had taken it, knowing he couldn't, and wouldn't, protest his sacking, unfair as it was.

"I can't help it," the owner, Mr. Huang had said. "The police tell me you've been babysitting kids and letting guests use the computer . . . I can't have this going on here, Feng. I need people I can trust."

Yeah, Mr. Huang. Fuck you, too.

He walked into the café opposite Russell's building and took a seat at the table just inside the window. Coffee smelled good. Today he'd even splurge on sweet rolls. The waitress kept running by him with other orders. She ignored him.

"Excuse me," he said.

She rushed by again. It was as if she couldn't see him. How rude! He stood and waved, knowing she could see him, but she didn't acknowledge him. He was stunned. A young Chinese couple came in and sat beside him at his table. They chatted away in Mandarin, as if they couldn't see him.

The woman was upset they'd lost their traveler's checks. The man was blaming her.

"Hello?" he said. "Can you see me?"

He tried speaking English and Mandarin and only when the waitress stood right next to him, blocking him did he realize . . .

Holy shit, I'm invisible.

Outside the café, he absorbed this shocking revelation. How was this possible? Was it true? He could see his reflection in mirrors and windows. He took a deep breath. The street noises hurt all his senses. He turned and looked across the road at his parents' apartment. This would be the test.

He crossed over, right between cars that should have hit him . . . hurt him. The bus he walked in front of should have *killed* him.

It didn't.

Holy shit. This is . . . unreal.

He wasn't sure how he felt about this. What if it was permanent?

Feng kept walking to his parents' place, aware how shabby it looked. He passed right through the locked gate, walked up the sagging wooden stairs and found the backdoor open. His father was in the kitchen, looking in the fridge.

"Hey, Dad," he said.

Nothing. Dad shut the fridge door. He had a black eye.

Probably mom socked him at some point. She often lashed out when she was drunk.

"Mei," he shouted. "We just have bananas. You want a banana omelet? There are two eggs left."

"Okay," she said.

Feng walked into the living room. His mom was on the sofa watching *The View*.

"Hey, Mom," he said. She kept staring at the bottom of her empty bottle of beer.

"We got any beer in the fridge?"

"No," his father shouted back to her.

"You'll have to ask Feng for some money."

His father came to the door and stared at her, a spatula in his hand.

"I tried calling him. He isn't answering."

"Try again. Little bastard that he is." She picked up her bottle and upended it into her mouth.

His dad shrugged.

"It's no use. He doesn't answer."

"Leave a message," Mom shouted.

"Already did."

Feng grew tired of their domestic squabbles and walked outside. He sat on the back steps in the sun. He opened his backpack, not entirely surprised to find that his *Banpaia* novel was gone.

Now what? He was hungry and thirsty, but not really. He had the same responses he'd always had, but heightened. He was here but not here.

And then he saw him.

Feng stared down at the young man who was staring up at him. He recognized the guy from some place but couldn't think where.

"Do you . . . can you see me?" Feng asked him.

Slowly, the guy nodded.

Feng ran down the stairs, through the metal gate and to the man. For a moment they stared at one another, then hugged.

"I've been alone for three days," the other man said.

"What's your name?"

"Vincent."

Vincent! "I heard about you. You were walking across the street with your friend—"

"Joby," Vincent said.

"Right. And you vanished."

"I was so depressed and *Banpaia* just . . . took me away."

Vincent's expression turned dreamy. "What do you think is going to happen to us?"

"I have no idea. I have a feeling that whatever might happen, will take place on Halloween."

"You didn't read the novel?"

"I only glanced at it, read a few pages. I got it yesterday. I know he's hundreds of years old . . . there must be others like us, right?"

Vincent stared at him. "How many pages exactly did you read?"

"What?" Feng was in a state of shock. He tried to focus. "You mean . . . in the book?"

"Um . . ." Vincent nodded.

"Not far at all, a few pages at most. I told you I only just got it. Why?"

"You're right about Halloween. Something is supposed to happen on that night, but I don't know what."

Feng felt a shiver go up his spine.

"Do you crave coffee and stuff but can't get it?" he insisted.

"Yes! I tried ordering coffee and couldn't get the waitress to help me. Hey, do you find street noises deafening?"

"Yes!"

They walked around the corner together. No one looked at them. No one could see them!

44

"We can still have coffee and we can still eat. People don't see us though. Guess you noticed. According to the novel, there's a bunch of us hovering between two worlds."

"Really? A bunch? How much is a bunch?"

"I'm not sure. You're the first one I ran into. I watched you trying to get hit by the bus."

"Do you have the book?"

"No. You?"

Feng shook his head. "It's like it . . . just disappeared."

"Same thing happened to me," Vincent said as they entered a café. "Watch this." He went behind the counter, poured two cups of coffee and brought them to a table.

Feng watched, fascinated.

"Drink fast," he told him.

Feng didn't waste time asking why. He picked up the creamer jug, poured a little into his cup and sipped. It was hot. And absolutely delicious. Feng found himself rolling the taste of the coffee around his tongue. It was as if he could taste every aspect of every drop. He got a glimpse of sunshine and faces, coffee picking, roasting, machines, trucks . . . the very people whose efforts had gone into producing this single cup of coffee. He could feel, see, smell and taste them all.

"I know, I know . . ." Vincent said. "I was like that the first time, but hurry."

Feng shook himself out of his sensual reverie and sipped.

"I feel better," he said. "Not so . . ."

"Light of body and head?"

"Yeah, something like that."

A waitress appeared at their table as Feng put his half-drunk cup on the table.

"What the . . ." She literally scratched her head. "When did I leave these here?"

She picked up the cups, sweeping them off the table.

Vincent slid a couple of bucks under the creamer jug. Her

eyes lit up as she glanced over, noticed them and swiftly palmed them.

"Wow," Feng said. "You got it all figured out."

"Not yet," Vincent replied, covering Feng's hands with his. "Thank you for showing up. I was about to lose my mind."

They walked along Hill Street. They stopped and listened to people talking outside an old Cantonese-style café. Two other men had disappeared since Feng . . . wait . . . they were talking about Feng!

"Good kid. Father's pretty upset."

Upset? His father hadn't seemed upset when he'd been upstairs in the apartment.

He saw one of the men waving and Feng watched his dad crossing over the road to the men playing Mah-jongg outside the café.

"Any news?" they asked.

"No."

Feng stared at his father, whose eyes were red-rimmed.

"His boss fired him last night, thinking Feng had something to do with Mrs. Wei's murder . . . now he's feeling guilty because Feng's disappeared."

His father did look upset. Feng felt an odd mix of sadness and surprise.

"The cops called me," Feng's father said. "They say a Chinese tourist who checked out of the hotel yesterday is the one who killed her. They already arrested him."

His dad shook his head.

"I knew my boy couldn't do a thing like that. Laziest kid I ever met, but he's no homicidal maniac."

He's calling me lazy?

Feng was aware of the other men's startled expressions. His father kept walking, Feng watched him go into the grocery store. He would try and wheedle food from them but with Feng not around to cover the tab, he knew the storeowner would shoo him out of there.

A few seconds later, his dad emerged again, a scowl on his face.

"Your dad is about as lovely as mine," Vincent said, putting his arm around Feng's shoulder.

They left the men chattering and kept walking.

"What else did the novel say?" Feng asked him.

"I read about the mist at night."

"Yeah, what about that?"

Vincent stopped walking. "It's the souls of all the men he's laid claim to. We're living between two worlds, Feng. Not here, not there, you know, not dead, but not truly alive. It says the men start to show up one by one, but none can say what happened to them. That's what's strange. I remember what happened to me, don't you?"

"Hell yeah, he gave me the best night in the sack I've ever had."

Vincent laughed. "He'll be back for you tonight, trust me on that."

Feng grinned. "I can hardly wait. So . . . what else did the book say?"

Vincent sighed. "I didn't get any further than that. I was hoping you did. Oh, I know we're all supposed to lean on each other and reach out to one another . . . but for me . . . and I don't know about you, there can only be one. I think I am in love with him."

"Me, too," Feng said, feeling his heart twist with pain. "Wow . . . this is all so weird, yet so cool."

"Feng!"

Vincent glanced at him. Feng's heart pounded in his chest as he turned and saw Russell walking toward him.

"I knew it was you! I followed you."

Feng threw himself into Russell's arms, fighting off tears. In the back of his mind some horrible fate had lingered for his best friend.

"Russell," he said, and felt his friend's arms tighten around him. "Are you all right?"

"I'm not sure. Can you see me?"

"We can see you," said the other man, "but no one else can."

"Who is he?" Russell asked, releasing Feng from his embrace.

"This is Vincent," Feng replied.

Russell's eyes narrowed. "*He* took all three of us."

There was no need to name him. They all knew of whom Russell spoke.

"Did you read the book?" Vincent asked him.

Russell nodded. "Some."

"How much of it did you read?" Feng pressed.

"I got about halfway."

Vincent and Feng looked at each other. "That's further than either one of us," Vincent said.

"What is supposed to happen?" Feng asked him. "Something is supposed to happen on Halloween, isn't it?"

"Yes. That gives us only two days."

"For what?" Feng insisted.

"For him to decide which one he will choose."

"Yes, and there is no contest," a voice rang out.

The three men turned around on their heels to see Ki striding toward them. He bowed his head quite elegantly at each of them in turn. "I, unlike the three of you, did read the entire book," he announced with a dazzling smile.

Russell muttered something under his breath.

Ki threw back his head and laughed. "I dropped everything I was doing, compelled to read the pages, find the message between the lines. I am prepared. And he will choose me. So," he shrugged, "not to worry your little heads."

Feng was not impressed by his attitude and neither were

Russell and Vincent. "What do you know? How does it end?" Feng demanded.

Russell and Vincent crowded around Ki, all echoing the same.

"Okay, okay," he threw up his hands, laughing. "Since I am forced to be in your company, we might as well play nice together. Russell," he glanced at him, "let's retire to your abode."

"Retire to my abode," Russell mocked, "what the hell has gotten into you, Ki?"

They followed along behind him as if he were the regent, and they his faithful followers.

Feng was about to put up a stink until Vincent put his mouth close to his ear and said, "Listen, unfortunately, Ki is the only one who has read the entire book, and he can tell us what we need to know, so for now, let's put up with his shit. Although I won't speak for you guys, after he spills it, all gloves are off!"

CHAPTER FOUR

No one had said anything for at least ten minutes. Feng now knew the true meaning of *the silence was deafening . . .*

There was a lot to think about. He wondered if at twenty-one he was ready to die . . . or if he was ready to live forever. And ultimately, it wasn't even his choice.

Banpaia.

He looked over now at Ki, and he envied him. He was so sure of what he wanted. Ki wanted to be with *him* forever!

So did Vincent.

It was only he and Russell who hadn't declared that they were willing to give him their lives. *Surrender their lives to him . . . to live with him eternally.*

A shiver ran down his spine.

Russell glanced at him and then moved closer.

"He'll come for you tonight."

"I know." And instinctively, he did know. He hadn't needed Vincent to tell him. And he was anticipating it eagerly, and that horrified him somehow. "The sex was . . ."

"Sublime," Ki supplied from across the room.

There was a resounding silence which confirmed that no one could have said it better.

Feng tilted his head and looked at Ki. "Aren't you afraid?"

"No. Why should I be afraid? It will only end badly for the three of you. Where I'm concerned, there will be no pain. There will only be eternal life with him . . . as his lover, his companion. I shall be his willing slave eternally."

"If he chooses you," Vincent snapped. "Your arrogance is astounding."

"I know him the best. I read the entire book. He gave me the time to read it all. That should be proof enough."

"That's means nothing," Russell commented.

Feng looked at him.

"Well, it doesn't," Russell protested.

"It's not that. It's just that I thought — "

"That I'd want to die? Feng," he moved closer, looked into his eyes, "that is the alternative. He has narrowed it down to the four of us. One of us will live forever, the rest of us . . ." He trailed off. "Well, you know how it ends."

"I don't understand why we aren't returned to life like the others who came out of the fog," Feng protested.

"We know too much now," Vincent supplied the reason.

"We have tasted heaven," Ki said. "How could any of you be content after that with an ordinary lover? It is more humane just to put you down."

"You son of a . . ." Russell growled. He made a lunge for Ki.

They fought and wrestled vigorously but none of the blows they exchanged had any impact.

"You might as well knock it off," Vincent told them. "You can never hurt each other. You are his candidates, and he will not allow any harm to come to us until he makes his choice."

Russell released Ki from where he had him pinned over the kitchen table. They both went back to their respective corners like two defeated boxers after the bell had been rung.

The hours ticked by and night fell. When the mist rolled in through the window, Feng lay stretched out on the sofa, dozing.

The first thing he felt was the cold, not ordinary cold. It was as if he'd been suddenly plunged into a freezer.

Feng took a sharp intake of breath, watching it hovering

heavily on the air as he exhaled. His entire body tingled. He rose from the sofa, peering around him. Then the mist began to thin, clear. "Russell, Vincent . . . Ki?" No answer. He knew instinctively that the three others were gone. He was . . . alone?

No. You are not alone. I am here.

Please. I don't want to die.

It doesn't matter what you don't want. Tell me what you do want.

You. I want you.

Do not lament, Feng.

Lament? Feng wiped at his face. Tears? He swallowed. *I know now.*

Yes. You know.

Feng felt his knees buckle. Suddenly strong arms swept him off his feet. Feng was surrounded, cradled, safe from all harm.

No one can hurt you here. You totally belong to me. Surrender.

Yes. Yes. Yes.

He was falling, his head hanging back. He hit the mattress. His shirt was unbuttoned, abandoned. His pants came next. Feng moaned as he felt his arms and legs extend out to his sides. He was levitating, and hands were moving over his flesh like a hundred soft feathers, spreading him open, reaching up inside of him, filling his mouth, his anus. *Oh God . . .*

Silent screams of ecstasy filled his mind as needle-sharp teeth sunk into his groin, sucking and licking. Then a hard body slid up over his, a face . . .

Feng gasped as he looked into those eyes, dark, deep, burning into his soul. He wanted to touch that face, beauty like he'd never seen overwhelmed him. A mouth slightly open temptingly close to his, lips moist with blood, two sharp, white incisors sparkling in the darkness of the room. *I love you.*

My precious Feng. You fill me with joy, your blood warms

me, reminds me of passions long ago.

Take me then. Choose me. At this moment he wanted to be his more that he could say. He didn't care about the cost, or the consequences. He only wanted to be *his*.

In the end, it isn't me who truly chooses. It is you. You come to me freely. And I know your heart.

Feng watched him, entranced, for although he spoke to him, his lips never moved, no actual words came from those moist, succulent lips. *I want to touch you. Please.*

Suddenly Feng felt his limbs move. The figure looming over him had vanished and for a heart stopping moment, Feng thought he'd gone. But then as he sat up in the dark room, he saw his silhouette standing in front of the window. Only the moonlight illuminated his shadow. He looked totally alone.

Tall, and muscular, in some ways, he resembled the carved statue of David, and as Feng came closer, reaching out to touch him, his skin felt cool to the touch, much like marble itself.

Aren't you afraid?

No. Why don't you speak to me, actually speak to me with your voice?

He turned around and gave him a sad smile. *It's better that I don't do that.*

God, he is so alone.

I am alone.

I hadn't meant . . . I mean . . .

You hadn't meant me to hear that. Those dark eyes burned into his own with the intensity of his gaze. You don't fear me. Yet you fear death. Feng, I am death.

Feng swallowed. The way you touch me doesn't feel like death.

Death can deceive. It is a thief in the night, which seduces then wipes everything out in its path without mercy.

Death is beauty.

It can be.

Feng bit his lip. The horror of his words echoed in the still of the night and he began to shake.

Your mother comes closer to death each time she poisons herself with the drink.

Feng's mouth gaped open. He took a step back but as he did, the room seemed to narrow, and *he* was just as close as before.

In her way, she flirts with death, makes love to it. And when she is saturated with the poison, it is death. The pain of life is far away and for that short while, it can't touch her. But she is weak, a child really. You are strong, Feng.

Then why me?

You called me to you. You all did.

I didn't. I . . .

No more now. Let me take you away from life for a little while longer. Like the drink, Feng, but remember there is a price. There is a price for everything.

Feng moaned as strong arms wrapped around him. Soft lips caressed his with tenderness. Moaning from somewhere resounded in his ears. Feng's hands moved over the smooth, hard marble. The coolness of his skin soothed his own fever-ish flesh.

They rolled there on the floor, kisses landed everywhere and then he was inside him, moving in a way that sent Feng to some beautiful place that resembled nothing he'd ever known.

The sharp teeth sliced into his throat and he clung to him, whimpering as he weakened, his body limp, the pleasure in-tense, floating away on a cloud. *Now you know death.*

Love. Love. Banpaia.

Someone was stroking his cheek. Feng's eyes fluttered open. You don't fear me. Yet you fear death . . . I am death . . .

I am death . . .

"Oh God," Feng gasped, bolting upright on the bed.

Russell placed a hand on his chest. "Whoa, whoa, Feng. It's okay. It's okay."

"Russell, Russell," Feng said. He grabbed him and hugged him close. *Now you know death . . . love . . . love . . .*

Feng clutched Russell tighter to him.

"Feng," he laughed a little, trying to loosen his hold. "You're cutting off my . . . I can't breathe."

Feng separated himself from Russell.

"Are you all right?" Russell asked him.

Feng suddenly noticed his state of undress and he drew the blanket up over him. "Yeah. I think so."

Russell smiled. "I never noticed how . . . ah . . . generously endowed you were before."

Feng blushed. "Yeah, well . . ." he muttered.

"No, I meant it, you . . . ah . . . have a stunning cock."

Feng looked at him, really looked at him. "Russell?"

"What?" He was staring into his eyes.

"Why didn't I notice before that we . . . I mean, you're everything I need."

Russell blushed a little. He glanced down at his hands. "I . . . we've always been friends and . . ."

"We should have been more," Feng whispered. Feng pushed the blanket off again.

Russell's hand moved up over his thigh, stroked the head of Feng's cock with his fingertips. "He won't allow it."

Feng smiled, nodded. "If we . . . if we manage to get out of this . . . then . . ."

Russell pulled him close this time, kissed his hair. "Yeah, I understand what you're saying." He pulled back, lifted the blanket back over Feng's lap. "So, did you learn anything more?"

"He's so alone. I can't quite explain it. It emanates from

him. And he knows everything about us."

"I know."

"I wonder how . . . he . . . I mean, he must have had someone with him before."

"Yes. According to what Ki told me, he had a companion but his search for a replacement has been long."

"Where did you all go when I was with him this time?"

"We found ourselves out in the mist."

"Did you find any others?"

"No. There are really only the four of us."

"What did Ki say about . . . him? Does he have a name?"

"Yes, he has a name, but no mortal may say it aloud. The book speaks of the companion but every two hundred years, he is compelled to seek another because that is the life span of the one he embraces. It is not eternal as Ki pretends. The one he chooses . . ."

"He does not choose," Feng interrupted, "the companion chooses him."

"What? I don't understand."

"He told me."

"*He* told you? You mean you actually had a conversation with him?"

"If you can call what we had, a conversation. It was . . ." Feng paused, "it was a little macabre and terrifying all at the same time, and yet . . . it was heart wrenchingly beautiful like a haunting love story."

Russell looked confused. "I don't . . . I don't really understand."

"I don't think I can truly make you understand. There are no words."

Suddenly Ki and Vincent strolled in. "So, I guess it's over," Ki announced.

"What is over?" Russell asked him as Feng stared at him curiously.

"The tryouts, and let's face it guys, when it comes to looks and," he twirled around, "physique, I'm afraid you guys are a little . . . lacking."

Feng shook his head. "You have it wrong I'm afraid. These are not tryouts like in a talent contest. He is exploring our souls more than our bodies. You are doing nothing for him sexually. You couldn't. He is giving you the pleasure and nourishing himself at the same time. There is no contest, Ki, except in your mind."

Ki laughed. "You have a great imagination. I shall put flowers on your grave, Feng, when I remember."

"My God," Feng said, "how could I have ever had a crush on you? You are so shallow and full of yourself. It is incredible."

"You have good taste, that's how," he winked.

"No, I was blind, looking only on the outside." Feng looked at Russell. "What I wanted was right under my eyes all along."

Russell smiled at him.

"Damn it, I regret it now," Feng said to Russell. "We would have been so great together. It's too late now."

Russell reached over and took Feng's hand.

"Oh, God, this is sick," Ki muttered.

Vincent smiled. "I think it's sweet."

"You would," Ki grunted and walked out of the room.

Feng reached out his other hand to Vincent and he came to join them on the bed. They all sat together quietly for a few minutes.

"Tomorrow night is Halloween," Vincent said suddenly.

"Tomorrow night? That's impossible. Where did all the time go?" Feng exclaimed.

"You've been sleeping for over twenty-four hours," Russell told him.

"Basically, it will come down to which one of us wants this

the most, right?" Russell looked at Feng.

"It comes down to which one of us is the weakest," Feng said softly.

"I don't understand," Vincent looked at him.

"It's a gift he gives to the one who can no longer cope with life, like a . . ." he swallowed, "like a drunk with the bottle." He closed his eyes.

"It's a kind of suicide then?" Russell gulped.

"I don't get it," Vincent interjected. "I know I have a shitty life, but Ki doesn't fit into this scenario. He has everything to live for. He's gorgeous, his family is rich and . . ."

"And, Ki is empty inside," Feng added. "We all are. The people around us are like . . . vampires," he whispered, "taking our love for granted, giving us nothing in return. So, we are hollow, too cowardly to find true love, craving relief from the pain."

The three of them sat there for the longest time with those words falling over them like repeated shovels full of earth over a grave.

Feng looked at Russell. How could he have missed it? All these years . . . now, after tonight, one of them could be . . . they all would be . . .

Banpaia . . . don't do this. I don't want to die. Don't take Russell. Please. I . . . love him.

"Vincent," Feng said, "can you . . . give us a minute?"

Vincent nodded.

When he'd left the room, Feng said, "I want to touch you, make love to you. Do you feel it?"

"Yes." His gaze settled on him. "I feel it."

"We can't. He won't allow us."

"I know." Russell pressed his forehead against Feng's. "It will be all right."

"We did this. This crazy world did this. Your parents, my parents, all of us, we brought him here. And we let the craziness swirl around us, take us, smother us, bruise our souls. We only had to fight. Now, it's too late, Russell . . . it's just too late."

The mist was everywhere. All Hallows Eve . . . the four men walked through the mist as if they owned it, while disguised children with their hand-held pumpkins raced along the streets in droves, squealing with delight as they compared their bounty. Weary adults trudged close behind, longing to return to their homes.

Squad cars patrolled the streets, and the fog thickened with every ticking minute.

"The parents are taking the kids home," Vincent said. "The fog is . . . getting worse."

Feng glanced up at the sky. The moon was now completely obscured by the mist.

Russell stood shoulder to shoulder with Feng. They held onto each other's hand. Vincent walked at their heels. He never did tell them his story, but Feng assumed it wasn't a pretty one.

Ki led them. And although he claimed to have no fear, his voice shook as he spoke, and at one time, he turned to Feng, his face filled with terror, and said, "I asked God to forgive me everything."

Feng narrowed his eyes. He wanted somehow to comfort him, his one show of vulnerability making him appear as a frightened child. But then just as Feng started to reach out to him, Ki put his mask back on again.

"He's coming," Ki said. "I feel it. I guess I should say good-bye to you all. Maybe I can talk him into sparing you, or at the very least, killing you swiftly, since I will be his mate."

"Ki, why don't you go and fuck yourself," Russell shot at him.

Feng's eyes widened as he looked at Russell, then he

grinned. It was appropriate.

Vincent laughed, too.

"You won't be laughing once he arrives . . ." Ki shot back. He stopped suddenly. His mouth froze in mid phrase.

The fog began to split in two, as if it were the Red Sea. And there he stood. *Banpaia.* The tall figure shrouded in a long dark cloak loomed closer as the fog thinned then receded behind him. His footsteps made no sound on the pavement. His beautiful, unlined face was without expression as he surveyed the three of them.

Ki stumbled toward him, shouting out something incoherent. He fell at his feet. "Master," he sobbed. "Take me."

Feng swallowed hard. His hand tightened in Russell's.

Banpaia's gaze settled on Feng.

"No," Russell whispered hoarsely. "Please no."

Feng felt Russell's hand slip away, as he was pulled forward. *Is it me?*

The mist rose again, and Feng felt strong arms lift him up. "Russell!" He looked around him to see only the fog and then he was rising with it, high above the landscape. *You lied. You said it was the one who wanted it most. Ki wanted it the most. He . . . please . . . Russell . . . don't hurt him.*

CHAPTER FIVE

There is no feeling more intrepid than opening your eyes and not knowing where you were, or who was going to jump out at you. *Am I still alive, or have I been transformed into some sort of . . .*

You are alive.

Where are you? Where are you, you . . . Feng sat up. He was laying on a huge, round bed with black satin sheets. The room was cool, but tastefully decorated. There were no windows.

He was naked, and the cold had caused goose flesh to form on his skin. He took the satin top sheet off the bed and wrapped it around him. There were no blankets.

Shivering, he crossed the floor to the door. He pulled on the handle and was surprised to see that it was open. When he stepped outside of it, he gasped. The corridor was very wide and long, door after door lined the way to the end where a huge stained-glass window spanned from ceiling to floor. There were no pictures, no mirrors, and no lights. The only light came through the stained glass which was done in a multicolored mosaic of shapes and shadows.

"Welcome to my home," a voice said. It sounded like an angel had spoken, deep, smooth, and hypnotic.

Feng turned, almost tripping on the sheet, and there he stood at the end of the hallway. He was dressed in black, his shirt open at the neck, the pants immaculate, without so much as a crease or a wrinkle and they fit tight to his body like a glove.

He was intoxicating, mesmerizing, so incredibly beautiful

that Feng could have sworn angels wept when they looked upon him.

"And yet, you don't want to stay with me."

Feng found himself looking into those eyes. A weakness claimed him. His mouth went dry.

"You know all I can give you and yet, you reject it."

"If you know that," Feng managed, "why am I here? You deceived me, led me to believe that it was truly a free choice to be with you."

"I didn't mean to deceive you, Feng. In fact, I told you the truth."

"It's like singing," Feng said, distracted by the tone of his voice.

"Would you prefer if I spoke in your head?"

"No. I . . . please . . . go on."

"It is the way it works. The way it has worked for centuries. But there is something about you. I broke the rule." He actually smiled as if he'd been very naughty and somehow that pleased him.

"Who . . . who enforces this rule?" And what have you done to Russell and the others?

"You needn't concern yourself with that." Russell and the others have not been harmed. They just don't remember.

They don't remember you.

They don't remember anything!

You mean . . . Feng narrowed his eyes. "Russell doesn't even remember I exist?"

He shook his head.

"And my parents?"

"You never existed, Feng."

Feng put his face over his hands.

Strong hands took them away. "I will not keep you here against your will."

Feng's eyes widened. "Then why did you bring me here?"

"In hope that you would change your mind." He put some distance between them.

"Where are we exactly?" Feng asked. "Does this place exist?"

"It does. We are in Tibet, in the mountains, one of my many homes. You will have all you need here. The servants have been told to cater to your every need."

"A blanket and some warm clothes would be appreciated."

He lowered his head. "Your wish is my command."

Feng had the irresistible urge to touch him. When he raised his head, Feng ran his fingers along his cheek bone. "What is your name? Will you ever tell me?"

"If you stay." He took Feng's hand, turned it over and kissed his palm. "You will stay here with me for a fortnight. After that time, you will make your decision. I will respect whatever decision you make." He released his hand. "The servants have prepared a meal for you in the dining room."

"Where is the . . ." He was gone. It was like he just disappeared in thin air . . ."dining room?"

Suddenly a short little man appeared. He looked like some sort of a monk, with his faded hassock on, and long braid hanging down his back.

He didn't speak. He motioned to him. Feng followed, trying not to trip on his sheet which he held tightly around him.

The servant opened the door to a large room with a long table. Flowers, candles, wine, and a roast of pork sat on the table. There was fruit and vegetables and a variety of sweets. It was a feast for a king.

He sat at the table and began to load his plate. He was famished and he was already on his second portion when he noticed him standing at the head of the table.

"Does it please you?"

He nodded with his mouth full. *It's so good. I was hungry.*

It's been a long time since I've tasted food. The smell of it, however, still delights me.

It is better when you speak in my head.

Less distracting. He smiled. The razor-sharp points of those teeth were suddenly apparent.

You almost forgot.

Yes.

I won't display them if they frighten you. He smiled again and they were no longer in view.

How did you become this?

It was bestowed on me at birth. I am the only one of my kind.

There are no more vampires?

I suppose there are, but I am far more than that. My only allowance is a companion. It saves me from madness.

Then you have a higher purpose.

I do.

What was he like, the last one?

He shrugged. "Troubled." He spoke aloud. "His life was misery. I embraced him and saved him from himself. I followed the rules."

Feng stood. He left the sheet behind. He came closer to him.

He turned, swept his body with his dark gaze.

"You never loved him."

"No."

"Have you loved them, any of them?"

"Yes."

"How many have you loved?" Feng looked up into his face.

"Only one. And he is truly not mine yet."

Feng's mouth opened. *Oh God. It is me.*

Yes. It is you, Feng. And I fear my heart will be broken this time. You love another.

"You can give me everything. You can give me a life longer than would be possible as a mortal, and physical pleasure which is beyond description, and yet I . . ."

He stroked his hair, lifted his chin and gently kissed Feng's mouth. "You are not willing to give up yet, but neither am I." The kiss held his mouth hostage, weakening any fight he might have possessed.

Passion erupted like hot lava searing his flesh and he gave himself over to it without a fight. The pleasure of his mouth on his was too sweet, the roaming of those cool, silky hands on his flesh so acutely satisfying, he cared not if he died at that moment. *This is unfair.*

Yes.

He laid him down on the table, on display much like the food had been before. And Feng watched as his host removed his black shirt and smartly fitted black pants, looking so like any mortal man, for a moment, he forgot what he was.

That intense gaze bore down on him, fearing nothing, missing nothing. He took his own erect organ in hand and stroked it slowly while Feng anticipated its path and moaned aloud.

He smiled. "Your pleasure is like blood to me. It intoxicates and seduces me. Arms up over your head, legs spread, bend the knees, rise."

And as he said these things, they were done. Feng found himself raised inches off the banquet table, his body in the position his lover prescribed.

That beauty hovered above him, his erection dragging over Feng's lips, fingertips massaging his jaw, tilting back his head. "Taste me," he urged.

Those words dripped with invitation, saturated themselves with sugar like candy from a stick and Feng opened to him.

The thick drops of fluid from his cock tasted like ambrosia and he opened wider and swallowed all he could.

Fingers massaged his throat and Feng took his wondrous cock deeper than he thought possible. The adrenalin rushed as he sucked and licked, and his cock pumped desperately between his legs.

The cock left him, still tantalizingly hard and solid. Feng licked his lips as a tongue moved over his throat, down his chest, tonguing both nipples, then nibbling his balls, the head of his cock, his legs forced high and almost over his head, thighs spread, a tongue explored deep inside his most intimate cavity.

Exposed. Open. Every inch of you is mine.

Feng sobbed with joy as every nerve in his being was stimulated, brought to live with his tongue, his fingers and then his cock.

"Fuck me! Oh yeah. Yeah. *Banpa . . . ia.*"

His cock was deep into his core. Was it possible for a cock to reach that depth? He was exciting his very soul. In. Out. In . . . . deep . . . . out . . . pounding . . . pumping . . . screaming . . .

"Yes, yes . . . do it. Do it . . . fuck me . . . deeper . . . deeper . . . .oh yeah. Yesssssss."

Feng wasn't sure how long he lay on that banquet table. He sat up eventually, stiff, his entire body aching from the exertion, and he was alone.

He took no blood.

No. I have other sources of food.

Feng sucked in some breath and got down off the table. "Where are you?"

Near.

You stay here always . . . in this place?

No. I will always be near you even when I'm far away.

That was incredible. I've never experienced anything like that.

It is a gift. It is all I have.

A sadness crept over Feng suddenly. He understood him. It was a message. Was he ready to give up his mortality for sex like that? When his cock was inside of him, his answer was a resounding yes! But now, when he was alone, he knew that had to be more.

Russell. Russell doesn't know me anymore. He's probably with someone else now. Feng wondered if he was allowed to leave here, would Russell know him or . . . maybe he'd be with someone else and his chance would have passed.

This was like a dream, but there was another side to it, a side filled with horror and death. "I don't want to die!"

He walked down the long, empty corridor. His words echoed off the walls. "To be in your arms forever is . . ." He swallowed hot tears. "I do love you . . . but not enough to give up on life yet. I'm sorry." The tears fell. He touched one and looked at his hand. The tear was tinged with pink. "What have you done to me?"

Silence.

"Where are you? What have you done to me? You told me I had the choice. You promised me that . . . you're a monster!"

Suddenly he appeared. He stood in front of the stained-glass window. "I have done nothing except maybe save you from every disease known to humanity including the common cold. You will live a long and healthy life, Feng."

"You fed me your blood."

He inclined his head.

"Knowing I wouldn't stay."

He gave him a faint smile. "I broke the rules. I have tried to make amends. I was hoping you'd change your mind, but I see now that your strength has carried you this far through a difficult life, and that it will continue to do just that."

"What about you," he could hardly speak. "What about your companion?"

"Hello Feng," a voice said.

Feng gasped. There stood Vincent. He was smiling, different. He was no longer mortal.

"Vincent was the natural choice. I have asked his

forgiveness."

Feng watched as Vincent moved closer to *Banpaia* and stroked his hair. He kissed his mouth, their tongues lingered together for a heart wrenching moment that made Feng feel a slash of jealously that he was unprepared for.

His host broke the contact. He reached out his hand. "I will take you home now."

"Come back soon," Vincent pleaded.

He smiled at him, nodded. Feng drew ever closer.

A long dark cloak flew around him and then he was encased in those strong arms.

The wind whipped around him, and the mist claimed them as he felt himself spinning out into nothingness. But there was no fear. Never any fear.

In an alley now, the long dark cloak pulled around his shoulders, he looked up into his face.

"You shall not see me again, Feng."

Feng felt himself break down inside, fragile pieces chipping off inside his heart. "But I shall remember you?"

He shook his head. "No." Those beautiful eyes were ablaze in the shadows. The moonlight played up the beauty of his face, the breadth of his shoulders.

"Can you not allow me one memory?"

He smiled faintly. "No. I'm sorry. I hope you have made the right choice."

Feng grabbed his hand. "I'm no longer sure."

"It's too late now, my love," he whispered. He came closer and kissed the top of his head. "You have a new life now. You must find it." He stepped back.

"Russell . . . my parents . . . they are . . ."

"Still alive but I took you out of existence. I cannot put you back."

"God," he put a hand over his mouth. "Then I am totally alone . . . like . . . like you?"

"I am no longer alone," he said. "Remember?"

"What if I need you?"

"You won't. You're strong. That's why you chose life over . . ."

"Over you."

"I will always love you, Feng," he whispered. "I know you were the one. Perhaps if I'd returned at another time." *You will hear my voice no more.*

Please . . . please . . . before you go . . . tell me your name. At least that . . . and let me remember it.

He stood some distance away. He turned his head.

Please, Banpaia. Tell me your name.

You must never speak it aloud.

I won't. I promise. Feng never removed his gaze from the figure who stood at the edge of the alley, desperate not to be deprived of his image for a second.

Suddenly, he looked right at Feng, and he said aloud in that heavenly voice. "Tenshi. My name is Tenshi."

Feng gasped. He went running down the alley but there was no one there. *Tenshi. Angel. His name was Angel.*

Feng walked out of the alley and as he turned the corner, he saw the Korean Café. He glanced down at himself, suddenly concerned about his attire. There was a long cloak hanging off his shoulders. Underneath he wore jeans and a t-shirt. He must have just come back from some Halloween party somewhere. He just couldn't remember where it was.

Russell. Who the hell is Russell? For some reason that name resonated in his head.

Feng walked into the café, slid into a booth, only realizing. He looked around at the patrons. Only one. "Russell?"

The young man looked up from his Manga comic.

"Hello?" He gave him an uncertain smile.

Feng got up and walked over to the table. He tightened the cloak around his shoulders. It suddenly warmed him, brought him great comfort. "My name is Feng. I had a dream about you."

"Me?" Russell met his gaze.

"Yeah." Feng smiled. "Can I join you?"

"Ah, sure, I guess. But ah . . . someone should tell you Halloween is over." He pointed to the cloak. "Great vamp coat you got there."

He nodded with a grin. "I think I was at a party. I don't remember."

"Must have been some party." Russell laughed.

"I really like *manga* too," Feng pointed to the comic as he sat down opposite him. "Can I buy you a cup of coffee?"

"Sure."

Feng lowering the cloak motioned to the waitress. "Two coffees, please."

She nodded.

"What's that one about?" Feng asked after the waitress came back with their steaming mugs.

"Rather unusual," he said.

"What's the title?"

"Lament of the Banpaia."

"What's it about?"

"This guy gets chosen as the great love of a *Banpaia* . . . but he's not the usual kind . . . he's kind of an angel, who swoops down every two hundred years to find a new mate. It's very romantic. The mortal guy is not ready to give up on life. He chooses his mortality and his mortal lover over the immortal."

"How does it turn out?"

"I don't know," he laughed. "The story isn't over yet. It's a little sad so far because the *Banpaia* breaks the rules for him. And he has to pay a penalty for that."

"Penalty. What's the penalty?" Feng held his breath.

"Are you all right?"

"I don't know. I just felt a little . . . please, tell me what the penalty is?"

"I'm not sure. I haven't read enough," he laughed. "Hey, you are really into this stuff. Want to come back to my place and read the rest?"

Feng nodded, smiled. "Yes."

"I love the illustrations in this one," Russell said as they walked along the street.

"Who is the artist?"

"Anonymous."

"Um," Feng smiled.

They walked up two flights of stairs and into a small, modest apartment. Russell made more coffee and they sat side by side on the sofa, glancing at the comic together.

"I feel like I've known you all my life," Russell said.

"Me, too," Feng took his hand.

"Oh, look at this one," Russell said, as Feng snuggled closer to him. "He has a cloak on like the one you were wearing. That's pretty neat!"

Feng peered closer. There was this beautiful man in a long black cloak. He stood in front of a stained-glass window, his head bowed. Feng traced his face with his finger. *Tenshi.*

Russell turned the page. "Oh my God, this is weird. Look at that guy. He looks . . . he looks like you!"

Feng's gasped. "It is . . . it is me."

"Maybe you know the illustrator."

"Maybe but . . . I . . ." He looked at Russell. Suddenly, he took the book from his hands and pulled it away. He threw it aside.

"Hey . . . what is it?" Russell laughed as Feng crawled on top of him and began to undo his shirt. "Make love to me, okay?"

Russell accepted his kisses without protest. Feng closed his eyes and savored the sensation of Russell's mouth moving down his chest. He paused to undo Feng's jeans and then lifted out his cock. "Magnificent," he said and smacked his lips. He took it into his mouth and began to lick and suck it from base to tip.

Feng let his head go back on the sofa. He let out a sigh of pleasure. A soft breeze blew through the window suddenly and Feng felt his heart thud in his chest. The comic blew open to the next page. A young man with a strong resemblance to him lay stretched out naked on a banquet table. A beautiful angel hovered, dark eyes caressing him. Feng gasped and moaned as he came in Russell's hot mouth. Tears stung his eyes as he stared at the picture, pleasure gripping his entire body.

Banpaia. Tenshi. Eternal love. Return to me.

ABOUT THE AUTHORS

A.J. Llewellyn is the author of almost three hundred published gay romance novels. A.J. lives in California, but dreams of living in Hawaii. Frequent trips to all the islands, bags of Kona coffee in the fridge and a healthy collection of Hawaiian records keep A.J. refueled.

A.J's passion for the islands led to writing a play about the last ruling monarch of Hawaii, Queen Lili'uokalani. A.J. has written a non-erotic novel about the overthrow of her kingdom written in diary form from her maid's point of view.

A.J. never lacks inspiration for male/male erotic romances and has to prise fingers from the computer keyboard to pursue other passions: collecting books on Hawaiiana, surfing and spending time with family, friends and animal companions.

D.J. Manly: I write not only for my own pleasure but for the pleasure of my readers. I can't remember a time in my life when I haven't written and told stories. When I'm not writing, I'm dreaming about writing, doing something wild and adventurous, or trying to make the world a better and more open-minded place to live in. I adore beautiful men, and I know I'm not alone in this! Eroticism between consenting adults, in all its many forms, is the icing on the cake of life!

D.J. has published well over two hundred novels/novellas and is a well-seasoned writer.